Why the Agouti
Has No Tail

FLOELLA BENJAMIN

Why the Agouti Has No Tail

and other stories

Illustrated by Jennifer Northway

Hutchinson

London Melbourne Sydney Auckland Johannesburg

Hutchinson Children's Books Ltd

An imprint of the Hutchinson Publishing Group

17–21 Conway Street, London W1P 6JD

Hutchinson Publishing Group (Australia) Pty Ltd
PO Box 496, 16–22 Church Street, Hawthorne, Melbourne,
Victoria 3122

Hutchinson Group (NZ) Ltd
32–34 View Road, PO Box 40–086, Glenfield, Auckland 10

Hutchinson Group (SA) Pty Ltd
PO Box 337, Bergvlei 2012, South Africa

First published 1984
© Floella Benjamin 1984
Illustrations © Jennifer Northway 1984

Set in Baskerville by Bookens, Saffron Walden, Essex

Printed and bound in Great Britain by Anchor Brendon Ltd,
Tiptree, Essex

ISBN 0 09 156800 5

Contents

Introduction

When I first tried to recall the stories I was told as a child in the West Indies, I really had to rack my brains to remember exactly how they went. I remembered all the characters, like Anansi the Spiderman, Dry Bones and the Agouti, but I had to ask my mum, who has a marvellous memory, to tell me the stories again. That's the beauty of traditional stories; they are handed down from generation to generation, with each family having its own slightly different version. So collecting the West Indian stories for the book was quite easy for me after all.

Gathering the stories from Africa, India and China was a bit more difficult – until I hit on a great idea: every time I saw a Chinese, African or Indian person in a bus queue, on a train, in the local shop, or in a restaurant, I would ask them to tell me the favourite story from their childhood. I must have listened to dozens of lovely stories from many people who were more than delighted to recall the traditional tales of their homeland. And I would like to thank them – especially the passengers of the Victoria line tube train where, one day, I had the whole carriage giving their versions of stories.

In this book I have tried to include the ones I liked best; some are well known, others less so. I had a lot of fun collecting and writing them, and I will be passing them down to my own son, Aston. I hope you enjoy them, too. Oh, and don't forget to pass them on. On and on!

Floella Benjamin

Why the Agouti Has No Tail

An agouti is a small animal that lives in the West Indies. It looks something like a squirrel, only it doesn't have a tail. A long time ago, however, the agouti did have a fine tail and this is the story of how it lost it.

Once upon a time the dog and the agouti were very good friends and lived together happily. One day Agouti and Dog were lazing in the garden, enjoying the afternoon sun when along came Goat, who was looking very pleased with himself.

'What are you so happy about?' asked Dog.

'I've been invited to a party,' replied Goat with satisfaction.

Now, both Dog and Agouti loved parties and when they heard this their ears pricked up.

'What party is this?' said Agouti. 'We want to come as well.'

'Oh, *you* can't come,' said Goat haughtily. 'This party is only for animals which have horns.' Then he trotted off with his head in the air.

Dog and Agouti looked at each other. Neither of them had horns and that meant that they would definitely not be going to the party.

'Oh, dear,' said Dog. 'I do love parties; there is always lots of food to eat.'

'This has spoilt my whole day,' said Agouti, and he went indoors to sulk.

The next day Dog and Agouti went into town. The news of the party had spread and everyone was talking about it, especially the animals with horns. Apparently, the party was to be held on a small island some distance away. There was to be a barbecue and lots of rum-punch to drink. All the horned animals were to leave for the island, by boat, the next morning and return in the evening after the party.

'It's not fair,' said Dog. 'I must find a way to go to the party.'

'But you don't have horns,' said Agouti. 'You would soon be spotted and then there would be trouble.'

'Don't worry, I will find a way,' said Dog, and he disappeared into the forest, leaving his friend Agouti behind.

Dog walked along a narrow path which led through the trees. He just had to think of a way to get invited to the party, but however hard he thought, he couldn't come up with any ideas.

Suddenly, as he rounded a corner, he saw a pile of old bones in front of him on the path. They were the remains of a cow that had died many years ago.

What luck, thought Dog, as he spotted a lovely pair of horns amongst the pile of bones. He picked them up and tied them to his head with a strong piece of vine. Then he rushed home to show his friend Agouti.

But Agouti was not very pleased when he saw Dog with the horns. 'It's all right for you. You are large enough to pass as a horned animal. But what about me? I would soon be spotted. There are no horned animals as small as I am. I still can't go to the party.' Agouti was more miserable than ever and he sat in a corner and sulked.

The next morning Dog was up bright and early. He tied the horns to his head as tightly as he could. 'Come down to the jetty with me, Agouti,' he pleaded, 'and see if my disguise works.'

Reluctantly, Agouti agreed. He was interested to see if Dog could get away with the deception.

The jetty was bustling with horned animals, all waiting for the boat to arrive and take them across to the island. So none of them noticed as Dog, wearing his horns, slipped quietly amongst them.

Agouti watched as Dog climbed aboard the boat and sat down next to Goat. His heart beat faster, as he realized that his best friend was going to get away with the trick and go to the party without him. He was so jealous that, before he could stop himself, he cried out, 'Stop! Stop! There is an imposter aboard.'

At this, all the horned animals looked at Dog and saw that he had tricked them. They picked him up angrily and threw him into the water.

When Agouti realized what his jealous betrayal had done, he turned and ran as fast as he could, with Dog close on his heels. He ran and ran as fast as his short legs could carry him, but Dog was angry and humiliated and soon caught up with Agouti, who scurried into a nearby hole. But Agouti wasn't quite fast enough and Dog snapped off his tail as he disappeared down the hole.

Well, needless to say, Dog and Agouti were no longer friends, and if you are ever in the West Indies and you see a dog scratching and barking at a hole, it is probably because there is an agouti down there. That is how the agouti lost its tail.

Akim the Mermaid

Once upon a time, in Africa, there lived a girl called Akim. She was very beautiful and kind, and many young men asked for her hand in marriage. But her parents wanted to make sure that the man she married was the right one for her.

Eventually, they decided on a young man who lived several villages away. He was brave and strong and came from a wealthy family. Although Akim had never met the young man, she felt sure he would be a good husband and she accepted her parents' decision without question. So, the marriage was arranged and a date set for the ceremony.

'It is the custom for the bride to go to her future husband alone,' said Akim's father. 'But, as you are going so far away, your younger sister will accompany you, so that you will have a friend to talk to when your husband is out hunting. You will also take a woman servant with you, to help with the cooking and cleaning in your new home.'

When the time came for Akim to leave, all the people of the village turned out to wave goodbye and wish her luck. Akim was sad to leave her home, but at least she had her sister and the servant woman to keep her company.

They walked all day, carrying their heavy bundles of belongings. Eventually, they came to a lake where they stopped to rest. 'The village is on the other side of this lake, mistress,' said the servant woman. 'Why don't you bathe and prepare yourself to meet your future husband?'

Akim thought this was a good idea, so she undressed and stepped into the cool, refreshing water.

Suddenly, the servant pushed Akim with all her might until she disappeared under the water, into the deepest part of the lake. Akim's little sister cried out and ran to the water's edge, but there was no sign of her sister. 'Why did you push her?' cried the little girl.

'Shut up, and listen to me! From now on, you will call me Akim. I will marry the man who was chosen by your parents. If you dare to tell anyone, I will push you into the lake as well!' said the wicked woman. 'You will be my servant now, and you will do exactly as I say or you will be sorry.'

The little girl was very frightened, so she did as she was told. Then the wicked servant put on Akim's clothes and together they went into the village, where the young man was anxiously waiting.

When he saw his bride he was a bit disappointed. He had been told that Akim was very gentle and kind. But when he looked at her, he thought she looked bad-tempered and disagreeable. However, the marriage had been agreed and he was a man of honour, so he married the wicked woman the next day.

He had built a fine house for his new wife to live in and the wicked woman lived there, waited on hand and foot by Akim's poor little sister, who was too frightened to tell anyone what had happened. The little sister worked hard from morning till night, cleaning and cooking, while the woman did nothing except shout orders at her.

'Go to the lake and fetch some water,' she shouted one day, 'and hurry back, or I will beat you!'

The young girl took the large water jar to the lake. When she reached the water's edge, she bent down to fill up the jar. Then, to her astonishment, she saw her sister Akim rising up from the depths to meet her. 'I thought you were drowned!' cried the little girl.

'I nearly was, but the kind Spirit of the Lake saw what that evil servant did and wouldn't let me die. Instead, I was turned into a mermaid. Look!' At this, she wriggled out of the water on to the bank.

Her sister was amazed at the long fish tail Akim had grown, but was overjoyed to see her dear sister alive. She told of the cruel servant woman and how she had masqueraded as Akim and had married the young man in her place. She also told of how she was forced to work every day as a servant.

When Akim heard this she was very angry, but there was little she could do as a mermaid. 'I will ask the Spirit of the Lake for help,' said Akim. 'Perhaps there is a way we can expose that servant's treachery. But, for the moment, you must say nothing of our meeting to anyone. Just go back to the village and carry on as before. Come here each morning so that we can be together.'

All this time, the husband had been feeling very miserable. The lovely woman he had hoped to marry had turned out to be cruel and selfish. She beat her young servant and never did any work herself. All she did was sit around all day and complain.

One day, when he was out hunting, he was feeling particularly downhearted. So he sat down by the side of the lake and gazed sadly into the water. 'Oh, I am so unhappy,' he sighed.

Suddenly, the surface of the lake rippled, and the man heard a voice. 'I am the Spirit of the Lake,' it said. 'You are the victim of a wicked trick. Your wife is not the girl you were supposed to marry.'

At this, the man jumped to his feet in astonishment. 'Then tell me, how I can find my true bride, O Spirit of the Lake!' he cried.

'Tomorrow morning, go to the side of the lake where

your wife's servant collects water, and hide in the bushes. Then you will discover the truth.'

The next morning he did as the Spirit had said. It wasn't long before Akim's sister arrived. He watched as she knelt by the water and cried out, 'Akim! Akim!'

After a short while, the most beautiful mermaid came up out of the water and slid on to the bank. He listened as the two girls talked of the wicked servant and how the Spirit of the Lake had promised to help them.

When he had heard enough, he jumped out of the bushes, knelt down beside the mermaid, took her hand and said, 'So you are the real Akim. You are as lovely as I was told. That evil woman will be punished for her crime, and you will be my true bride.'

When the Spirit of the Lake heard this, the spell was broken and Akim's tail disappeared.

'Oh, Akim,' cried her sister. 'How wonderful – you're back to normal again!' And they hugged and kissed each other with joy.

Then they went back to the village and told the story to the chief, who was very angry. 'Bring the wicked servant here!' he commanded.

The woman was dragged from her house and brought before the chief. When she saw Akim and her sister standing next to the man she had so cruelly tricked, she fell down and begged forgiveness.

'How do you want me to punish this woman?' the chief asked Akim. 'Should I have her thrown into the lake and drowned?'

But Akim was not a vengeful person. She asked only that the wicked woman should be driven from the village for ever, so that she could marry and take her rightful place beside her husband and live happily with him as his true bride.

How Anansi Got His Stories

Anansi the Spiderman came to the Caribbean from West Africa many years ago. But his adventures are still talked about in Africa. He is very clever and cunning, and he has a special gift that has made him famous: at the first sign of trouble or danger he can turn himself into a spider.

Anansi stories have not always been called Anansi stories: they were first known as Tiger stories. You see, Tiger was the most powerful of all animals and everyone in the forest respected him.

However, Anansi wanted the stories to be named after him. So, one evening, Anansi went to see Tiger, who was lying in the shade of a tree. Anansi gossiped for a while with Tiger until eventually he felt the time was right to ask his favour. Being very cunning, Anansi thought he would start by flattering Tiger.

'O magnificent Tiger, you are not only brave and strong but also wise and clever. Your fame has spread throughout the land, and everyone knows of you and respects you. But as for me, I am weak and insignificant. If only I had something to make people respect me and remember my name.'

Tiger enjoyed being flattered by Anansi and wanted to prove to all the animals what a clever ruler he was. So he turned regally to Anansi and said, 'Perhaps there is some way I can help make others remember your name.'

'Well, there is one favour I would like to ask of you,' said Anansi.

'What is it?' said Tiger. 'Speak out!'

'O brave, wise Tiger,' said Anansi, 'the stories we all know are named after you; but how wonderful it would be if they were named after me! Then everyone would remember my name.'

Tiger opened his eyes in surprise. He hadn't expected Anansi to ask such a big favour of him. He loved the stories and didn't want to lose them, but he felt he could not say no in front of all the animals which had gathered around. After all, he had offered to help Anansi.

Then he had an idea. 'Yes, Anansi, the stories will be yours, on one condition,' said Tiger. 'You must capture Snake, who lives down by the river, and bring him to me alive. If you complete this task, then the stories will be named after you.'

As Anansi wandered off to attempt his task, Tiger and the other animals laughed at the thought of Anansi the Spiderman capturing Snake, who was both strong and clever.

That night Anansi lay awake trying to think of a way to capture Snake. At last, he had a very clever idea and could hardly wait to try it out.

When the morning came, Anansi rushed down to the path that Snake usually took every day up from the river. He started to dig a deep hole and then placed an egg at the bottom of it. Anansi felt sure that when Snake passed by and saw the egg in the hole he would climb in to get it, for Snake loved eggs. Once inside, he would not be able to get out because of the steep sides Anansi had built.

Anansi hid in the bushes and waited for Snake to pass by. It wasn't long before Snake came slithering up the path and saw the hole with the egg in it. But Snake was no fool, and he did not climb into the hole; he simply coiled his long tail around an overhanging branch and slid his long body down into the hole to reach the egg, which he swallowed in one!

Oh, dear, thought Anansi, Snake is much cleverer than I thought. I will have to try another plan to catch him.

This time Anansi built a cage from bamboo sticks and placed a ripe, juicy calabash mango inside. Then he left the door of the cage open and waited, ready to slam it shut once Snake was inside. But Anansi had not made the cage big enough, and Snake put just his head inside the cage and ate up the juicy mango.

Once again Anansi had failed. It looked as if he would never have the stories named after him. He sat miserably by the river, thinking what to do next. Then he noticed Monkey fishing and it gave him an idea . . . .

He ran home, found a piece of rope, and made a noose at one end. He put the noose on the ground, covered it with leaves, and on top he placed a piece of goat meat which his wife had cooked for dinner that night. Then he sat on the branch of a tree nearby, holding the other end of the rope, and waited patiently for Snake to come past.

At last along came Snake, who spotted the meat and, sure enough, began to eat it. Quietly above, Anansi waited for the right moment to pull the noose tight around Snake's head. Then suddenly he tugged on the rope as hard as he could; but Snake was much heavier than he had expected and the next thing he knew he had landed in a heap beside him.

'So, Anansi,' said Snake, 'it's you who has been trying to trap me all week. You'd better have a good reason for it, or I will swallow you up.'

'Oh, please don't, I beg of you,' pleaded the bruised Anansi. 'I do have a good reason, but now I'm sure to lose my bet.'

'What bet is this?' asked Snake curiously.

'I have a bet with Tiger,' said Anansi, 'that you are the longest creature in the forest. Even longer than the tallest bamboo tree over there.'

'You are quite right,' said Snake. 'I am the longest creature in the forest. You win your bet.'

'But how can I prove it to Tiger?' said Anansi.

'That's easy,' said Snake. 'Cut down the bamboo and put it beside me and you will see.'

This was just what Anansi wanted Snake to say. He hurried off to the nearby bamboo grove, cut down the longest bamboo shoot he could find, and rushed back to where Snake was waiting. Snake immediately stretched out beside the bamboo.

'There you are,' said Snake proudly. 'Am I not longer than the bamboo?'

'Mmmm, not quite,' said Anansi, 'but if you stretch as hard as you can you will be longer and then I will win my bet.'

'How's that?' asked Snake, stretching as hard as he could.

'Well,' said Anansi, 'you are so long I cannot watch your head and tail at the same time.'

'Then tie my head to the bamboo,' said Snake, 'and then go to the other end of the stick and watch my tail.'

'OK,' said Anansi, as he excitedly tied Snake's head to the stick and rushed down to the other end. 'Come on! Stretch! Stretch!' he shouted. 'You are nearly there – just a bit more.'

Snake gave one last push and at that moment Anansi seized the opportunity to tie Snake's tail to the stick as well.

'Well, I never, Anansi's done it! He's captured Snake alive,' shouted all the animals in amazement, as Anansi passed them by, carrying Snake to Tiger.

Tiger was surprised, too, that Anansi had captured Snake alive, and he had to keep his word.

'Well done, Anansi,' said Tiger, 'you are clever and cunning and deserve to have the stories named after you.'

And that's how the stories of Anansi the Spiderman came to be.

Why Thunder
and Lightning Live
in the Sky

Many, many years ago Thunder and Lightning lived on earth like everyone else. Lightning was young and quick-tempered and caused his mother Thunder much distress.

No one liked either of them very much because of their noisy, troublesome ways. If Lightning didn't like someone he would fly into a violent temper, striking out in every direction and destroying everything in sight. Whenever Thunder saw what her son was doing she would call out loudly to him to cease. But her voice was so loud that it shook the earth and frightened the villagers.

Everyone became very tired of Lightning's violent outbursts, which were always followed by his mother's deafening shouting. So they decided to complain to the king, who decreed that Thunder and Lightning must leave and live on the outskirts of the village where they would annoy no one.

This worked for a short while, but soon Lightning was back to his old ways, burning, killing and generally causing trouble, always closely followed by his mother rebuking him in her loud, thundering voice.

Once more the villagers went to the king, who decided that Thunder and Lightning should move even further away to the distant mountains, and he ordered them never to return to the village again. Thunder and Lightning didn't like being exiled; they rumbled and flashed

angrily as they left and they could be heard complaining for weeks afterwards.

It was not long, however, before Lightning returned. He had been plotting his revenge and he showed no mercy as he set fire to the dry crops, causing bush fires to rage and farm houses to burn to the ground. Of course his mother chased after him, bellowing at him to stop, but he took no notice of her and continued to wreak his revenge.

But this time Lightning had gone too far. The villagers felt they could no longer endure his spiteful and wicked ways, and they demanded that he and his mother be banished from the face of the earth. So the king ordered that they be sent to live in the sky where they could do no more harm.

When Thunder and Lightning heard what their punishment was to be, they begged and pleaded for forgiveness, promising never to disturb anyone again. But the people no longer trusted them, for they had broken their promises before. So the king asked all the birds – the parakeets and cockatoos from the forest, the flamingos from the lakes, the eagles from the mountains and the vultures from the deserts – to come and pick up Thunder and Lightning and fly them high up into the sky, which was to be their new home. The birds were only too pleased to help, for they too were fed up with the noisy, inconsiderate pair.

So hundreds of birds flocked around Thunder and Lightning and picked them up with their claws and beaks. They flew them up and up into the sky until they were high above the clouds, and there they left them.

Everyone thought the birds had finally taken Thunder and Lightning to a place so far away that they would never disturb anyone again.

But this was not quite the case, because even now we

still get visits from them, with Lightning losing his temper and sending bolts of fire down to the earth, and the deafening voice of his mother, Thunder, never very far behind.

Listen out for them next time there is a storm.

Fee Fee Foo

There was once a king who had three beautiful daughters. They were so precious to him that he never allowed them to leave the palace grounds to play with the other children. The girls were so well guarded that no one outside the palace even knew their names.

The king thought himself very clever to have kept the names of his daughters so secret, and he decided to hold a grand competition to see if anyone could guess what they were. He offered a prize of as much gold as the winner could carry away from the palace, and this attracted people from all over the kingdom; but no one managed to guess even one of the names, never mind all three.

When Anansi heard about the competition he decided that he would try to win the prize, but being Anansi he thought of a crafty way to find out the girls' names.

That afternoon, while the girls were out playing in the palace grounds, Anansi slipped into the palace, carrying three lovely bunches of flowers. He crept past the guards and up the stairs to the three sisters' bedroom and he placed a bunch of flowers on each of their beds. Then he hid in the cupboard and waited. When the girls returned that evening and saw the pretty flowers, the youngest said, 'Oh, look, Fee Fee Foo and Sugar Blossom, look at these beautiful flowers. Who could have left them?'

'Who indeed, Tinky Tangle?' said the other two. 'Let's go and ask our father if it was him.' And they picked up the flowers and went to show the king.

When he heard them go, Anansi came out of the cupboard, climbed out of the window and over the palace wall, and ran home as fast as he could.

The next morning he called on Rat, Goat, Donkey, Hare and Dog and told them to collect their steel drums and meet him at his house as quickly as they could. When they were all assembled Anansi led them towards the king's palace.

'Why are we going to the palace with our steel drums?' asked Goat. 'We have already tried to guess the names of the king's daughters and failed.'

'Ah,' said Anansi, '*I* have not yet failed, and if you do as I say we will all soon be rich!'

When they reached the palace gates, Anansi told his friends to play a calypso rhythm on their steel drums and he began to sing:

> 'Tinky Tangle, Sugar Blossom
> And Fee Fee Foo,
> Where are you?
> Where are you?'

'Now join in!' shouted Anansi to his friends, and they all marched into the courtyard singing the calypso:

> 'Tinky Tangle, Sugar Blossom
> And Fee Fee Foo,
> Where are you?
> Where are you?'

When the king heard the sweet music, he came out into the courtyard to listen, for he loved a good calypso. But when he heard the words, he realized that someone had guessed the names of his daughters.

Then he spotted Anansi. 'I might have known it would be you, Anansi!' he cried. 'I don't know how you did it,

but you and your friends are the winners; take as much gold as you can each carry.'

Rat, Goat, Donkey, Hare and Dog all looked at Anansi with joy and amazement. Now they realized why he had asked them to bring their steel drums! They ran through the palace filling them to the brims with gold, then they happily struggled home under the weight of their newly won treasure.

From that day on, the king allowed his three daughters to play with other children, who would come to the gate and sing:

> 'Tinky Tangle, Sugar Blossom
> And Fee Fee Foo,
> Where are you?
> Where are you?'

And Tinky Tangle, Sugar Blossom and Fee Fee Foo would answer:

> 'Here we are, here we are,
> Happy to play with you.
> Tinky Tangle, Sugar Blossom
> And Fee Fee Foo.'

They were happy now, for they had lots of new friends to play with, thanks to Anansi.

The Mouse Who Wanted
to Be King

A long time ago, in India, there lived a little mouse – just an ordinary mouse with brown fur and long whiskers. He lived under the floorboards of a house in the poorest part of the city and he had to search hard for scraps of food to eat.

One day the mouse was sitting underneath the verandah of the house, where it was cool and shaded from the hot midday sun, when he heard a commotion going on in the street. He peeped his head out to see what was happening and saw a great procession of magnificent elephants passing by. Riding in a gilded basket on the back of the most splendid elephant was the king.

The king was dressed in beautiful robes of red silk, embroidered with gold. On his head he wore a turban into which were sewn rubies and pearls, and on his feet he wore sandals of the finest leather.

When the little mouse saw the king and all his finery, he said, 'If only I were king, I could wear silken robes and jewels instead of dull brown fur. I could live in a palace and eat the finest food instead of living under the floorboards where I have to scratch for crumbs.'

All that night the little mouse lay awake thinking about what he had seen. Then, just as the sun was coming up, he had a wonderful idea. He marched round to the cloth merchant and demanded to see the owner.

'I am the Mouse King,' he said. 'Give me some of your

finest red silk cloth or I will tell my subjects, the rats and mice of the city, to come to your shop and gnaw holes in all your cloth!'

The cloth merchant was so afraid of rats and mice invading his shop that he did as the mouse asked and gave him some of the material.

The mouse took the piece of cloth to the tailor, who was busy making a coat with the help of his children. When they saw the little mouse they all stopped work.

'I am the Mouse King,' said the little mouse. 'Make me a fine robe from this cloth or I will command my subjects, the rats and mice of the city, to invade your shop and gnaw holes in all your suits and coats.'

This so frightened the tailor and his children that they started work on the tiny robes immediately, while the mouse waited impatiently.

Soon the garment was finished and the mouse put his fine robes on. He stood in front of the mirror and admired himself; he walked up and down trying to be as king-like as he could. He made such a funny sight that the tailor's children could hardly stop themselves giggling.

The mouse took a long piece of the cloth and wound it around his head like a turban, then he strode off towards the cobbler, who was sitting cross-legged in his shop hammering a pair of shoes. When he saw the strange little mouse in his silk robes and turban, he stopped work and said, 'What can I do for you, little mouse?'

'I am the Mouse King and I command you to make for me a fine pair of sandals from the softest leather you have,' said the mouse grandly. 'If you refuse, I will tell all my subjects, the rats and mice of the city, to invade your shop and gnaw at all your leather.'

The cobbler thought the mouse looked very funny in his robes and could hardly stop himself from bursting out with laughter. But he decided that he had better do as the mouse asked, for he did not want hundreds of rats and mice to gnaw at his leather.

Very soon the mouse had a lovely pair of sandals made from the softest leather the cobbler could find. The mouse put on his new sandals and strutted up and down the street in them. Now I look like a king, he said to himself. He did not see the people in the street laughing at the funny little mouse in his fine clothes.

The next day the mouse put on his new clothes and set off for the king's palace. He walked up to the gates, which were guarded by two soldiers. 'Stand aside,' he ordered. 'I am the Mouse King and I am here to see your ruler!'

The soldiers looked at the little mouse in his fine robes and could hardly believe their eyes. 'Of course, Your Highness,' said one of them, trying not to laugh, 'follow me.'

The soldier led the mouse to the throne room where the king sat on a great golden throne. The soldier marched up to the steps which led up to the throne and bowed. 'Your Majesty,' he said in a loud voice so that everyone in the huge room could hear, 'you have a royal visitor. May I present His Royal Highness, King Mouse!'

There was a stunned silence as the little mouse walked boldly up to the throne. 'Greetings, O King,' he said. 'I have come with a proposition for you.'

The mouse took his time, stroking his whiskers once or twice before he spoke. 'If you do not give me half your kingdom at once, I will command all my subjects, the rats and mice of the city, to invade your palace and destroy it!'

At this, the king stopped smiling and a look of anger came over his face. 'How dare you come here and threaten me,' he bellowed. 'I have a good mind to order my palace cat to chase you away.'

As he spoke, a huge white cat appeared from behind

the throne and leapt towards the poor little mouse, who squeaked in terror and scampered up on to a nearby table, shaking with fright as the cat fiercely swished its tail from side to side.

Just then the king's little daughter, who had been sitting on her father's knee, said, 'Oh, father, he is such a funny little mouse with his silk robes and sandals, let me keep him as a pet.'

Now, the king loved his little girl more than anything in the whole world and it gave him great joy to see her happy, so he snapped his fingers and the fierce cat went back to its basket behind the throne. A cage was brought and the little mouse was put inside.

'Oh, thank you, father,' said the princess. 'I shall look after the little Mouse King and feed him on scraps from the royal kitchens every day, and I shall make him a bed of soft straw to sleep on.'

So, you see, the mouse *did* get to live in a palace after all and he never had to scratch around for food again.

Dry Bones' Party

Dry Bones lived by himself on top of a mountain, where none of the animals ever went. It was a very dry and barren place, not suitable for anything except Dry Bones. He would spend his days alone, cackling and rattling around the mountainside, discouraging anyone from coming near.

Then one day, to the animals' surprise, word spread that Dry Bones had invited them all to a party where, he promised, there would be plenty to eat and drink.

Now, the animals did not like Dry Bones, but they loved a good party, especially if there was plenty of food. So when the day of the party arrived, all the animals turned up. They couldn't believe their eyes when they saw the table laden with delicious food.

Soon the party was in full swing and everyone was enjoying themselves – except Monkey. He knew Dry Bones hated all the animals and liked being alone, and he was curious as to why he was suddenly being so kind to them.

While all the other animals were eating and having a good time, Monkey noticed Dry Bones quietly slip out of the room. So he followed him round to the back of the house to see what he was up to. At the back of the house Dry Bones had built a fire, and on the fire was the biggest cooking pot Monkey had ever seen.

Monkey climbed on to the roof of the house and

looked into the pot to see what Dry Bones was cooking. But when he looked down, he saw that there was nothing in the pot but boiling water. As Dry Bones stirred the pot, he started to cackle in his croaky voice:

'More bones for Dry Bones,
More bones for Dry Bones.
Fat bones, juicy bones,
More bones for Dry Bones
Tonight . . . Ha! Ha! Ha!'

Then, to his horror, Monkey realized that he and all his friends were in great danger. Dry Bones *did* have a reason for inviting them all to the party. They were to end up in the pot!

Monkey knew he had to warn his friends, who were all having a great time inside. He rushed back into the party, screeching and chattering at the top of his voice: 'Run! Run! Run for your lives!'

At first everyone was too busy enjoying themselves to take any notice of Monkey, and anyway he was always screaming and chattering about something or other.

When Monkey saw that no one was paying attention to him, he jumped on the table, sending cups and plates and food flying, which made everyone stop and look at him in amazement. 'Run! Run for your lives, everyone!' screamed Monkey. 'The party is a trap. Dry Bones has plans for a feast of his own. And that feast is us! Run! Run now!'

At this, all the animals scattered in every direction. Through the doors and windows they jumped and scurried, then down the mountainside they ran as fast as they could, with Dry Bones rattling behind them. Finally, when all the animals had reached the safety of the forest and had disappeared into their hiding places, they chanted back up the mountain:

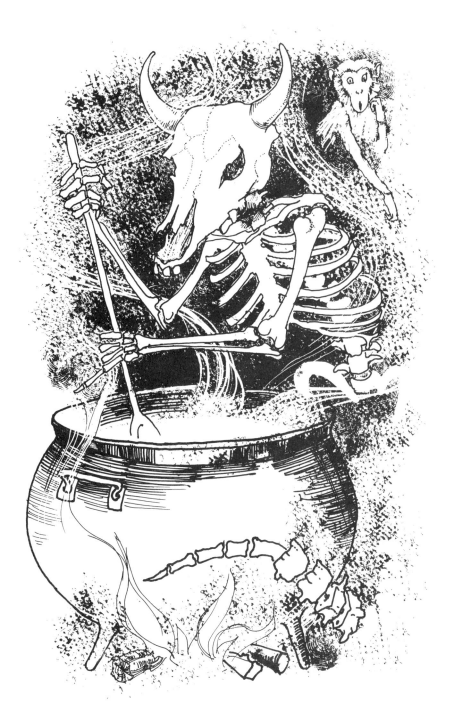

'No bones for Dry Bones,
No bones for Dry Bones.
No fat or juicy bones,
No bones for Dry Bones
Tonight.'

When Dry Bones heard the animals taunting him with their chant, he covered his ears and stamped his feet in anger, for he knew he had lost them and had nothing to show for his night's work. Dry Bones was so angry that you could hear the echo of his bones rattling as he returned to his mountaintop empty-handed and swearing never, ever to have a party again.

'I will have to think of another way to get their bones,' he cackled, and he started to mutter:

'More bones for Dry Bones,
More bones for Dry Bones.
Fat bones, juicy bones,
More bones for Dry Bones,
But not tonight!'

The Crow and the Sparrow

One day the crow and the sparrow decided to have a curry dinner together. The sparrow provided the rice and the crow brought the meat for the dish.

The sparrow was a really good cook, and while she prepared the meal, Crow waited anxiously for his share. Sparrow laid the food out beautifully on the table, which she had decorated with flowers.

When they were about to sit down to eat, Sparrow looked at Crow and exclaimed, 'Goodness me, you are not going to sit down to dinner without washing, are you? Your beak and claws are so dirty. Go and wash them at once.'

Crow was really hungry and did not think he was that dirty, but he thought it was best not to argue with Sparrow, for even though she was small, she was very bossy. So off he hurriedly flew to the nearest stream and said:

'Your name is Stream,
My name is Crow.
Please give me some water,
    For if you do so,
I can wash beak and feet
And the nice curry eat;
Though I really don't know
    What the sparrow can mean,

For I'm sure, as crows go,
   I'm really quite clean!'

'Of course you may have some,' said the stream, 'but first you must go to the deer, borrow one of his antlers and use it to dig a small hole, into which the water can flow.'

So off Crow hurriedly flew to find a deer, to whom he said:

'Your name is Deer,
My name is Crow.
Lend me an antler,
   For if you do so,
I can dig a small hole
   For the water to flow;
Then I'll wash beak and feet
And the nice curry eat;
Though I really don't know
   What the sparrow can mean,
For I'm sure, as crows go,
   I'm really quite clean!'

'Of course I will,' said the deer, 'but first go to the cow and ask for some milk for me to drink. Then, by all means, you may borrow my antler.'

So off flew Crow to find a cow, to whom he said:

'Your name is Cow,
My name is Crow.
Please give me some milk,
   For if you do so,
The antler is mine,
   To dig a small hole
   To be my wash bowl;
Then I'll wash beak and feet
And the nice curry eat;
Though I really don't know

42

What the sparrow can mean,
For I'm sure, as crows go,
I'm really quite clean!'

'Of course I will,' said the cow, 'but first I need some grass to eat, so that I can make you some milk. Fetch me some, please and milk is yours.'

So off flew Crow to a field and said:

'Your name is Field,
My name is Crow.
Please give me some grass,
   For if you do so,
   Madam Cow will give milk
And the Deer, sleek as silk,
   Will lend me his antler
   To dig a small hole
   To be my wash bowl;
Then I'll wash beak and feet
And the nice curry eat;
Though I really don't know
   What the sparrow can mean,
For I'm sure, as crows go,
   I'm really quite clean!'

The field replied, 'Of course you may have some grass, but you will need a scythe to cut it down. Go to the blacksmith and ask him to make one.'

So off flew Crow to the blacksmith and said:

'Your name is Smith,
My name is Crow.
Please make me a scythe,
   For if you do so,
The grass I can mow
As food for the cow,
Who will give me some milk

For the deer, sleek as silk,
Who will lend me his antler
To dig a small hole
To be my wash bowl;
Then I'll wash beak and feet
And the nice curry eat;
Though I really don't know
What the sparrow can mean,
For I'm sure, as crows go,
I'm really quite clean!'

'Of course I will,' said the blacksmith, 'but I will need your help to fan the flames of my forge, with your wings.'

So Crow began to flap his wings, and the coals in the forge grew red hot and the blacksmith made him a scythe.

Crow thanked the blacksmith and flew back to the field and cut some grass, which he gave to the cow, who gave him some milk, which he gave to the deer, in return for his antler, which he took to the stream and used to dig a small hole, into which the water flowed. Then he flew back to Sparrow.

But when he got there, he found that Sparrow had not only eaten her share, but also his share of the lovely curry.

'You took so long,' said Sparrow, 'that I thought you weren't coming back. So I ate all the curry. I'm sorry.'

Crow was so angry and hungry that he vowed never to have a wash again.

That is why crows are black all over, even today.

Why Anansi the Spiderman Makes Webs

One day Anansi got together with his friends Hare and Rat, and planted a field of sweet potatoes. They dug the ground, planted the sweet potatoes in neat lines, and waited for them to grow. Every day they would go to the field and pull out any weeds that tried to choke the tender young shoots. Of course, Anansi always made some excuse as to why he couldn't work, and usually spent the day lazing on the grass watching Hare and Rat working in the hot sun.

Eventually, the time approached when the crop could be harvested, and Hare and Rat arranged to meet Anansi the next morning at the field. That night, though, Anansi crept down to the field and dug up some of the sweet potatoes, put them in a sack, and hid it near his home.

In the morning when the three met, Hare and Rat noticed that part of the field had been freshly dug, but Anansi pretended not to notice. As usual, Anansi made an excuse, saying he had a sore back and couldn't work, and sat down to rest in the shade. While they worked, Hare and Rat decided that they would watch the field that night to see if the thief returned

When half the field had been harvested, Hare and Rat decided to call it a day. They waved goodbye to Anansi and said that they hoped his back would be better in the morning so that he could help with the work. As soon as he was out of sight, Hare and Rat ran back to the field and

hid themselves in a bush. After a few hours they began to think that they were wasting their time.

'No thief is foolish enough to return to the scene of his crime so soon,' said Hare. 'Let's go home, I'm tired.'

'Maybe you're right,' said Rat. 'Let's forget it.'

But just as they were about to leave they spotted a shadowy figure approaching. 'Quick, hide,' said Hare. 'We'll catch him in the act.'

So they ducked down behind the bush again and watched as the figure started to dig up the sweet potatoes. Then they crept quietly towards him. When they were right behind him, Rat shouted, 'Caught you, you miserable thief!' At this, the robber spun round in surprise.

'ANANSI!' cried Hare. 'You are the thief!'

Hare and Rat were both so surprised that Anansi had time to make a run for it, but they soon recovered themselves and gave chase.

Before long Hare and Rat started to gain on Anansi, who wasn't a very fast runner. He looked over his shoulder and saw Hare and Rat close behind, and he knew that if they caught him he would be in serious trouble. But just then he saw a large tree ahead and he leapt up into the branches and clambered up to the top, where he sat, trembling with fear. Hare and Rat couldn't climb trees so they stood at the bottom looking up angrily at him. 'You wait, Anansi,' said Rat. 'When you come down, we'll give you what for.'

But Anansi had no intention of coming down; he just changed himself into a spider, as he always did when he was in trouble or danger.

'You will have to come down eventually,' shouted Rat. 'You can't stay up there forever without food.'

When morning came, Rat went home for a rest, leaving Hare to guard the tree. Later he returned to allow Hare to go home for a while.

From his branch Anansi watched these comings and goings with dismay. His stomach began to rumble and he looked around for something to eat; but the tree was bare. Oh, why didn't I choose a mango tree to climb, instead of this old stump, he thought.

As the hours passed Anansi grew more and more worried. He even considered giving himself up, but Hare and Rat were still very angry with him and he soon thought better of it. There must be something I can eat, Anansi said to himself. Then he spotted a few flies buzzing around nearby, and to the starving Anansi even they began to look delicious. So he thought up a way to catch them by spinning a web, and that is why spiders still weave webs to this day.

Eventually, Hare and Rat got fed up with waiting at the bottom of the tree and told Anansi they would forgive him as long as he promised never to steal from them again.

The Mean Pear Seller

Once upon a time, in China, it was customary for traders to set up their stalls outside the gates of large cities where they would sell their wares to passing travellers.

One such trader was a pear seller. He was a very mean man and would charge the hungry travellers high prices for his juicy pears. At the end of the day, as the city gates were about to close, a crowd of poor people would gather around the stalls and the traders would give them any fruit or vegetables that had not been sold; but the pear seller never gave anything away.

One day, as the pear seller sat by his stall, he noticed an old man standing looking at him. The old man was dressed in rags and was obviously very poor.

'Please give me a pear,' said the old beggar.

'Go away, you filthy old man. If you want a pear, then you must pay for it like anyone else,' said the pear seller.

'But I have no money; all I ask for is one pear. I have not eaten all day,' replied the beggar.

At this, the pear seller became very angry because the old man was beginning to attract a crowd. 'Go away, I tell you!' he shouted. 'If I gave every beggar a pear I would soon be poor myself.'

Now, standing in the crowd was a young man, who, although poor himself, felt sorry for the old man. 'Here you are, old friend,' he said, tossing him a coin. 'I'll pay for your pear.'

The old man picked up a pear and ate it. When he had finished, he said to the young man, 'Thank you for your kindness, young sir. Now please allow me to show my gratitude.'

At this, he took a pip from the core of the pear and threw it to the ground. The crowd watched as he covered it with earth and spoke a few words under his breath.

Almost at once a small green shoot appeared. It grew rapidly, and within a few minutes it had become a small pear tree laden with ripe, juicy fruit. The crowd of onlookers clapped and cheered with admiration at the old beggar's magical tree and were even more delighted when he told them to help themselves to the fruit. When all the pears were picked, the tree disappeared back into the ground as quickly as it had arrived.

Now, all this time the mean pear seller had been watching the display of magic, and he thought of a way he might be able to profit from it. As the crowd of people dispersed, shaking their heads in amazement and carrying armfuls of pears home, he went over to the old man, who was sitting by the roadside, smiling to himself.

'Oh, wise old wizard,' said the crafty trader, 'you have taught us all a lesson here today. You proved that it is best to be kind and charitable, for anyone who is will be rewarded tenfold.'

'That is correct,' said the old man. 'You have learnt the lesson well.'

The cunning pear seller looked humbly at the ground and said, 'Then perhaps you could show me the trick, so that I may teach others the same lesson.'

At this, the old beggar laughed out loud. 'Take a look at your stall, pear seller! It looks as though you do not need tricks to show people the meaning of kindness.'

When the mean pear seller looked at his stall, he saw that there was not a single pear left on it. You see, the old man's magic had only made the crowd *think* they had seen a pear tree grow from a pip – the pears were really from the mean pear seller's stall.

The rest was just an illusion . . . .

The Fish Prince

Once upon a time there was a powerful rajah, who lived in a splendid palace with his wife, the ranee. The rajah and ranee were loved by the people, for they were good and generous, and it was a cause of great sorrow to everyone that their beloved rulers had no children. Everyone prayed to the Gods to bless the couple with a child, but sadly the prayers were not answered.

One day some fish were delivered to the royal kitchen to be cooked for the rajah's dinner. Amongst them was one little fish that was not dead. One of the kitchen-maids took pity on the little fish and put him in a bowl of water. Shortly afterwards, the ranee saw him and decided to keep the pretty fish as a pet. And because she had no children, she lavished all her affection on the fish and loved him as a son. When the word spread that the ranee kept a fish and loved him like a son, the people named the fish 'Muchie Rajah' (the Fish Prince).

Soon Muchie Rajah grew too big to live in the small bowl, so the ranee instructed one of her craftsmen to make an ornate tub for him to live in. In time, however, Muchie Rajah grew too big for even the tub to hold him. So, sparing no expense, the rajah ordered a great pool to be constructed in the palace grounds. When it was finished, it had steep sides, forty feet high, from which there projected a balcony, where the ranee would sit and toss tasty morsels of food to Muchie Rajah. Sometimes she would sit there all day, watching the great fish swimming round and round in the pool.

'How lonely you look, my son,' she said one day. 'I will find you a wife.'

So the ranee sent her messengers out to find a bride for the Fish Prince. They went all over the kingdom, asking everyone if they would allow one of their children to marry Muchie Rajah; but they all answered; 'We cannot give one of our dear little daughters to be married to that great fish – even though he is Muchie Rajah.'

When she heard this, the ranee became even more determined to find a wife for her son, no matter what the cost. So she offered a bag of gold to anyone who would allow their daughter to become the Muchie Ranee (the Fish Princess). But not even the poorest people were tempted to sell their children.

At last the news reached the ears of a woman who lived on the very edge of the kingdom. Now, this woman had married for a second time, her first husband having died. She had a daughter by her first marriage and her new husband also had a daughter by a previous marriage. The woman hated her step-daughter and tried, by every means in her power, to make life unpleasant for the girl. She gave her the hardest work to do and the least food to eat.

When the woman heard that there was a large reward being offered for a girl to marry the Fish Prince, she called for the ranee's messengers. 'Give me the gold and you can take my step-daughter to marry the Muchie Rajah,' she said to them.

Then, turning to the girl, she said, 'Go down to the river and wash your saree, so that you will look clean and presentable for the Muchie Rajah.'

The girl did as she was told and went to the river, where she cried bitterly at the thought of being married to the Fish Prince.

As she cried, her sobs were heard by an old cobra who lived in the river bank. When he saw the girl crying, the cobra said to her, 'Young girl, why are you crying?'

'Oh, Cobra,' she answered, 'my cruel step-mother has sold me to be the wife of the Muchie Rajah, that great fish.'

'Do not be afraid,' said the cobra, who was very wise. 'Pick up three stones from the river bank and tie them up in the corner of your saree. The Muchie Rajah whose wife you are to be, is not really a fish, but a real prince who was turned into a fish by a wicked sorcerer. Be prepared, and as soon as you see him, throw the first stone at him; he will then sink to the bottom of his pool. The second time he comes, throw the second stone and he will sink to the bottom of the pool again. When he rises for the third time, throw the third stone and he will resume his human form.'

So the girl carefully tied three stones up in the corner of her saree, waved goodbye to the cobra, and went back to where the ranee's messengers were waiting to take her to the palace.

When they arrived there, the ranee was waiting impatiently, but when she saw the girl, she was most pleased. 'You are very pretty, my dear,' she said. 'You will make my son, Muchie Rajah, a fine wife. You will meet him immediately.'

The girl was taken to the great pool and lowered down the side to a ledge which was level with the surface of the water, and there she was left alone for the night.

She looked at the dark, deep water that lay at her feet, and waited. After a few moments, the surface of the pool was disturbed and she could see the great fish swimming towards her at great speed. As he grew closer, he lifted his head clear of the water and opened his huge mouth. The girl, although terrified, took hold of the first stone and

hurled it at the fish with all her might. No sooner had she done so than Muchie Rajah sank to the bottom of the pool and everything fell silent. The girl waited, breathlessly, her heart pounding against her chest.

Then suddenly the great fish rose again, almost beside where she stood. She hardly had time to throw the second stone, but somehow she did, and the fish sank once again. The girl held the last stone in her hand.

So far everything had happened just as the cobra had said it would. She knew that the fish would approach her again and that she must not fail with the last throw.

Then, without warning, there he was, his great body almost out of the water. As he towered above her, she threw the last stone with all her strength. There was a blinding flash, and there, standing before her on the ledge, was a handsome prince.

The poor girl was so exhausted by her frightening ordeal that she fell to her knees, crying. But the handsome prince knelt down beside her and said, 'Do not cry; you have broken the spell and I am free. Will you marry me and be my princess?'

The next morning the ranee came to her balcony to see how the Muchie Rajah liked his new wife, and she was very surprised to see the handsome young prince standing by the pool with the girl. She ordered that they be raised from the ledge immediately and when she heard their story she was overjoyed.

The news spread throughout the land and the people rejoiced, because they now had a prince and princess. Even though the prince was no longer a fish, the people still called him Muchie Rajah (the Fish Prince), and his wife, the Muchie Ranee (the Fish Princess).

Sun and Moon's Party

Long, long ago Sun, Moon and Water all lived happily on earth together and were all great friends. Sun and Moon loved to visit Water's house, where all three of them would gossip and tell amusing stories to each other.

One day, when Sun and Moon were on one of their regular visits to Water's house, they said to him: 'You have never been to our house. We would love you and your family to visit us, so that we can return the hospitality you have shown us. Surely that's what friends are for.'

'We would love to come and visit you,' said Water, 'but we are afraid that if we came it would mean that you would have to leave your home.'

'But why?' said Sun and Moon.

'Well,' said Water, 'I do not know how to tell you this . . . but your house is too small to hold us all.'

'Oh!' said Sun. 'But it just so happens that we are building a much larger house. When it's finished, will you then come?'

'If it's large enough, of course we will come,' said Water, 'but do keep in mind that my family takes up a lot of room and we would hate to come to your house and damage anything.'

Sun and Moon were overjoyed to hear that Water had finally agreed to visit their home. They worked hard, night and day, to finish their spacious new house. Then they sent an invitation to Water, which read:

> Sun and Moon
> have pleasure in inviting
> Water and all his family
> to visit their new home
> for tea.
>
> (Please come)

Water felt sure that the house, no matter how big it was, could not hold all of them, but he did not have the heart to refuse his good friends' invitation. So he accepted and began to flow in with his family and the friends who lived with him: in came thousands of fish, hundreds of whales and dolphins and even turtles.

When just a few of them had arrived, Water said, 'Are you sure you still want all of us to come in? We are bound to fill your house to the brim.'

'Of course you are all welcome. There's plenty of room for everyone,' said Sun and Moon.

'Very well,' said Water, and in he and his family poured. Soon Water had risen so high that Sun and Moon had to move to the highest part of their house to avoid getting wet.

'There are lots more of us to arrive yet,' shouted Water. 'Do you still think your house is big enough for us all?'

'We can't go back on our word now,' whispered Sun and Moon to each other. 'We will just have to move up to the sky to make room for Water and all his family and friends.'

So that's what they did, and the party is still going on today, with Sun and Moon high up in the sky looking down at their friend Water.

The Tree House

Once upon a time, in Africa, there were three boys who lived with their father. Sadly their mother had died, so their father had to look after them on his own, which wasn't very easy because he had to go out every day to work on his farm.

While he worked, the father worried about his three little boys, for there were many dangerous wild animals that prowled the nearby forest, not to mention the evil people who would like to steal the three boys away and make them work like servants.

One day the father had an idea. He went into the forest to look for a tall tree, and after searching for a while he found one that was perfect. His plan was to build a house high up in its branches where his boys would be safe from the animals and the wicked people.

First of all, he found some strong vines; he carefully knotted these into a long rope ladder which he rolled up and slung over his shoulder. Then, with his sharp axe tucked into his belt, he slowly climbed the tree. As he went, he chopped off each branch until he was at the top of the tree and the trunk was smooth and free from footholds. Now no one would be able to climb the tree, and the only way up or down was by the rope ladder which he tied securely to a strong branch and lowered down to the ground.

Having done this, he climbed down again and began

collecting logs with which to build the tree house. He tied them into bundles and pulled them up with a long vine, and in this way he carefully built a lovely little house high up in the wide branches of the tree. When he had finished, he climbed down the ladder and looked up into the branches. It was perfect; he could hardly tell there was a house up there, so well was it hidden in the thick foilage.

The man was very pleased with his work and went to fetch his three children at once. When they saw their new home, the boys were delighted and they quickly settled themselves in for their first night in the tree house. They pulled up the ladder and felt safe and secure amongst the branches which swayed gently in the breeze.

The next morning their father got ready to go to work, but before he left he told them what they must do: 'When I have climbed down the ladder, you must pull it up at once. Do not let it down for anyone except me when I return tonight.'

'How will we know you have returned, father?' asked one of the boys. 'We cannot see the ground below, for the leaves are too thick.'

This was a problem the man had not thought of and for a moment he was puzzled. Then he had an idea. 'I've got it!' he said. 'I will say a little rhyme, and when you hear it you will know it is safe to lower the ladder.'

'What is the rhyme?' cried the boys excitedly.

'Now let me think,' said their father. 'I know! I will call my three boys who love to play, *tree* boys! So, sons, listen. This will be the rhyme:

> Three boys, tree boys,
> Your playing now stop,
> Your father is home, so
> The ladder please drop.'

At this, the boys' father set off for work. He climbed down the ladder and as soon as he reached the ground the boys pulled it back up again. 'Remember,' called their father once more, 'do not lower the ladder for anyone but me,' and he disappeared into the bush.

Every morning their father would go off to work and every evening he would return and say the little rhyme and the ladder would be lowered. While he was away the boys were happy in the tree house; they played amongst the wide branches, and the birds which lived in the tree soon grew accustomed to them and would fly into the house and sing prettily as the boys fed them crumbs from the table.

As time passed the boys grew bigger, and one day their father said to them, 'Soon you will be big enough to come to the farm and help me.' The boys were excited at the prospect of going to work with their father and eagerly awaited the day when they would be allowed to do so. 'Maybe next month,' said their father. 'But until then things will remain as they are.' So he climbed down the ladder and watched as they pulled it back up, before setting off to work.

What he didn't see was a pair of sinister eyes watching from the bushes. The eyes belonged to an old crone who lived all alone in the forest – some people said she was a witch and stayed well away from her. She had noticed the goings-on up in the tree and could catch the occasional glimpse of the three strong young boys as they played amongst the branches. How nice it would be if I could catch those three lads and make them work in my field, she thought. I would soon have crops to sell and I would grow rich. But the old hag could see no way of getting up the tree except by the rope ladder which the boys had pulled up.

Then she had an idea. I know, she cackled to herself, I

will pretend to have a message from the boys' father and get them to lower the ladder so that I can climb up and capture them. She went to the foot of the tree and called out: 'Yoohoo, yoohoo, I have a message from your father; lower the ladder so that I may climb up and give it to you.'

When they heard the woman calling, the boys stopped playing and listened. 'That is not our father,' said one. 'We must not lower the ladder to anyone but him.' So they just called down, 'What is the message? We can hear you, so there is no need for you to come up.'

The old woman knew her trick had failed and without answering she ran off into the bushes.

That evening, when the boys' father returned, he called out as usual:

> 'Three boys, tree boys,
> Your playing now stop,
> Your father is home, so
> The ladder please drop.'

He didn't see the old woman hiding in the bushes listening to the rhyme.

Ah, she hissed to herself, so that is the secret of how to get those boys to lower the ladder. I will be back tomorrow and then we shall see what we shall see. Hee! Hee! Hee!

When the boys told their father about the old woman, he said, 'You did well, my boys. Now you understand why we have to be so careful. The woman was lying about the message and would no doubt have captured you if you had lowered the ladder.'

The next morning the old crone waited until their father had left for work, and watched as the boys pulled the ladder up. Then she went to the bottom of the tree and said:

'Three boys, tree boys,
Your playing now stop,
Your father is home, so
The ladder please drop.'

When the boys heard this, they stopped playing. 'That's odd,' said one. 'Our father has returned from work very soon and he sounds so strange. Perhaps there is something wrong. Let's lower the ladder and let him come up.'

But the eldest boy was not sure, and he called down: 'We cannot hear you; please say the rhyme again, father.'

So the woman called out as loud as she could:

'Three boys, tree boys,
Your playing now stop,
Your father is home, so
The ladder please drop.'

'That is not our father,' said the eldest boy. 'It is that wicked old woman who tried to trick us yesterday. Go away!' he shouted. 'We are not that easily fooled; that is not the voice of our father.'

When the old woman heard this she was furious and shook her fist at the boys as she stormed off into the forest. 'I'll be back,' she shouted as she went.

When she returned to her house, she sat down in front of her cooking pot to think. 'There is only one way I can get those boys to let that ladder down,' she muttered. 'I must make my voice sound like their father's.' So she set about mixing a magic potion that would make her voice as deep as a man's. She put everything she needed into the cooking pot and stirred the mixture round and round as it bubbled over the fire. The ingredients were the most horrible things like frogs' eyes and lizards' tongues, but

the old woman was so determined to catch the boys that she didn't care.

When the potion was ready, she closed her eyes and drank the horrid liquid down with one gulp; it tasted so nasty that she almost fainted. But as soon as she recovered she tried out her voice to see if the potion had worked and, sure enough, when she opened her mouth to speak, out came a gruff, deep voice just like the boys' father's. Straight away she rushed back to the place where the tree house was, stood at the bottom of the tree and said:

'Three boys, tree boys,
Your playing now stop,
Your father is home, so
The ladder please drop.'

The three boys listened carefully to the voice saying the rhyme, then the middle boy said, 'That is our father home from work – let the ladder down.' So the three boys lowered the ladder – and the old crone climbed up it.

When she reached the tree house, she grabbed the poor boys before they had a chance to recover from the shock of seeing the horrible old crone instead of their father. 'Got you!' she said in her deep voice. 'Your days of playing are over; now you will come and work for me.' Then she tied the boys up and carried them down one by one to the ground below, before marching them off into the forest to her house.

When the boys' father arrived soon afterwards, he knew straightaway that there was something wrong: the ladder was still hanging down from the tree and there was no sign of his three boys. He searched in the nearby bush, but they were nowhere to be seen. Then he remembered what the boys had told him about the old woman who had pretended to have a message from him for them. It must be her, said the boys' father to himself. People say she is a witch. She must have used a spell to trick my boys.

He ran as fast as he could to the nearby village and went straight to the chief's hut. The chief was very troubled by what he heard and sent a messenger to fetch the wise old man who lived on the edge of the village. When the wise man heard what had happened, he shook his head.

'I know this woman,' he said. 'She is a wicked witch and it will not be easy to rescue your sons, for she knows some pretty powerful spells. But there is a way that her magic power can be broken.'

'Tell me what it is,' said the boys' father. 'I will do anything to save my sons.'

'Well,' said the old man, 'if you can manage to get hold of the wooden stick she always carries with her, and break it in two, her powers will be broken as well. But I warn you – if she finds out what you are up to she will put a terrible spell on you, so you had better be careful.'

The man thanked the chief and the wise old man and set off to find the witch.

By now it was growing dark and the forest was full of strange sounds as he made his way to where the old crone was said to live.

Presently, he came to a clearing with a small hut in the middle of it. Inside there was a fire burning and he could see the shadow of someone inside moving about. He crept closer and managed to crawl to the open doorway without being seen. Cautiously he peered inside, and there, sitting with their feet and hands tightly bound, were his three sons. The old witch was sitting at the table eating her supper, and leaning against the arm of the chair was her long magic stick. But as the man looked at the stick he realized that he would not be able to grab hold of it quickly enough to prevent the witch putting a spell on him. He would have to think of a clever plan to get closer to it.

He crept silently away into the bushes and ran back to the tree house, where he thought for a while. Then an idea came to him. He took some ashes from the fireplace and rubbed them into his hair to make it look grey. Then he found an old blanket and wrapped it around himself. Next, he took his most valuable possession from its secret hiding place. It was a small golden drum which his father had given to him and which had been in his family for generations. He tied it around his neck with a leather cord so that it hung on his chest. Finally he climbed back down the ladder and broke off a dry branch from another tree to use as a walking stick. He was now ready to put his plan into action and set off back to the witch's house.

As he got close to the clearing where the witch lived, he began to lean heavily on the walking stick like an old man, and with his other hand he held the blanket tightly around him.

The three boys were all asleep in the corner of the hut and the witch was sitting in her favourite chair, smoking a pipe and thinking of work for them to do the next day, when there was a knock on the door. 'Who is that knocking at my door at this time of the night?' she screeched. 'Whoever it is will be sorry!'

She picked up her magic stick and went to the door to see who was foolish enough to disturb her. Standing in the doorway was a grey-haired old man with his eyes closed, leaning on a walking stick.

'What do you want?' hissed the witch.

'Have you a bowl of soup for a blind old man? I have walked many miles today and I am half starved.'

'You can starve to death for all I care,' said the witch. 'Now be gone before I put a spell on you.'

'Oh, please help me,' said the old man. He held out his hand and let the old blanket he had wrapped around him fall open. There around his neck hung the golden drum.

When she saw the gold shining in the moonlight, the old woman's eyes lit up. More gold for my collection, she thought to herself, and it will be easy to steal from this blind old fool.

'Come in, old man, of course I've a bowl of soup for you. Come in and sit yourself down.'

The old man felt his way into the hut and sat down at the table while the witch busied herself at the stove. She thought the old man was blind, of course, and that he couldn't therefore see her sprinkle a powerful magic sleeping potion into the bowl of soup.

'Here you are. I hope you enjoy it,' said the witch with a sly smile, as she handed the old man a bowl of soup. One spoonful of that, she thought to herself, and you will fall into a deep sleep and the gold will be mine.

'Thank you kindly,' said the blind man, and he took a spoonful of the soup. But as the woman looked away for a second he quickly threw it under the table. 'Mmm, this soup is delicious,' he said, 'but I feel very tired all of a sudden. May I lie down in front of the fire and sleep?'

The wicked witch thought her evil plot had worked. She looked at the golden drum eagerly and could hardly wait to get her greedy hands on it.

'Of course you may,' she said, as she helped the old man over to the warm hearth. As soon as he lay down, the old man pretended to fall into a deep sleep and made loud snoring noises.

After a few moments, when the witch felt sure he was soundly asleep, she stealthily knelt down beside him and reached out to untie the cord which was around his neck. Then, all of a sudden, to the witch's surprise, the old man sprang to his feet and grabbed her magic stick. The witch was so shocked that she couldn't even think of a spell to cast. She just sat on the floor with her mouth wide open, and before she had time to gather her wits, the man broke the stick in two across his knee.

There was a flash of light and a noise like the rushing of the wind, which woke up the three sleeping boys in the corner of the room. To their astonishment they saw the old witch slowly crumble into a pile of dust on the floor of the hut, and they couldn't believe their eyes when they saw their father take off the old blanket and shake the grey ash from his hair.

'Oh, father!' they cried. 'We knew you would come and rescue us from the wicked witch.'

'Yes, my sons,' he said, 'you're safe now and she can never harm anyone ever again.'

Their father untied the three boys and they all made their way back to the tree house, where they all lived happily together for a very long time.

Kisander and Her Pomsitae Tree

Kisander the cat had a lovely Pomsitae tree in her garden, with dozens of ripe, juicy pomsitaes hanging in its branches.

Every day, as he passed Kisander's house, Anansi would look over the garden fence at the delicious fruit and wish he could get his hands on it. But Anansi was afraid of Kisander. She was clever and had sharp claws; she could move silently through the forest and could see in the dark. How could he get those pomsitaes, while she was guarding her tree?

As the days passed, Anansi grew more and more desperate to eat the pomsitaes. Finally, he decided to try to steal some, no matter what the danger.

That evening Anansi watched Kisander as she swung in her hammock under the pomsitae tree. Eventually, she went inside and Anansi waited until he thought she was asleep. Then, stealthily, he scaled the fence and crept over to the tree. He climbed up into the branches and quietly started to pick the pomsitaes, which he put into the sack he was carrying. There were so many ripe, juicy pomsitaes that Anansi soon forgot himself and got quite carried away with greed. He began crashing about in the branches noisily. Mmm ... here's a nice one, and another, said Anansi to himself.

It wasn't long before Kisander, who had been sleeping soundly, was rudely awakened by the rustling and mutter-

ing outside her window, and she threw open the door and hissed, 'Who is in my tree, stealing my pomsitaes?'

Anansi was so startled by this that he dropped the sack, which fell down and landed with a thump at the foot of the tree.

'Aha,' cried Kisander. 'There goes the thief,' and she pounced at the sack.

When she saw it was a sack full of pomsitaes, she looked up into the branches above and called out, 'Come down at once, thief!' But as she looked up, with her bright, piercing eyes, she could not see Anansi, because he had changed into a spider, as he always did when he was in danger.

'The thief must have escaped,' said Kisander. 'But at least he has saved me the trouble of picking my pomsitaes.' She picked up the sack and went indoors. But she could not get back to sleep and she paced to and fro restlessly, glancing occasionally out of the window at her garden.

Anansi sat uncomfortably on a branch, trembling with fright. Sometimes he could see Kisander's eyes flashing through the window as she looked up at the tree, but luckily she did not spot him. Then, to make matters worse, it began to rain and Anansi huddled on his branch shivering miserably. There was not even a single pomsitae left on the tree for him to eat, for they were all in the sack he had dropped, so his stomach rumbled with hunger.

Finally, Kisander went back to bed, but it was dawn before Anansi plucked up the courage to come down from the tree and run home as fast as his legs would carry him.

From that day on, Anansi couldn't even look at a pomsitae without remembering his ordeal in Kisander's tree.

Tiger Son

Once upon a time there was a woman who lived with her only son in a small town in China. One day the son was on a journey through the mountains when he was attacked and eaten by a tiger. When his mother heard the sad news, she was beside herself with grief. Her only son was dead and now she was alone with no one to look after her.

Soon her grief turned to anger and she decided that the tiger that had committed this crime should be caught and punished. So she went to the magistrate and asked him to make out a warrant for the tiger's arrest.

When the magistrate heard the woman's request, however, he fell about laughing. 'We can't arrest a tiger,' he said, 'and even if we could, how would we know which tiger to arrest? There are dozens of them in the mountains around here.'

But the woman was so upset that no amount of reasoning could calm her down. 'You are the magistrate,' she cried, 'and a murder has been committed; it is your duty to see that justice is done.'

The people who had gathered around nodded in agreement. 'She's got a point there,' one of them shouted, and everyone laughed. The magistrate shifted uncomfortably in his seat. He could see no other way out of this awkward situation but to issue a warrant for the tiger's arrest, so he took out his pen and wrote out the document. At this, the woman and the crowd were satisfied and went about their business.

Now, every morning the warrants that had been issued by the magistrate the day before landed on the desk of the chief of police and he would assign one of his constables to each case. When he saw the warrant for the tiger's arrest he thought someone was playing a joke on him. 'Arrest a tiger, indeed!' he snorted. But then he had an idea; he would carry the joke one step further. There was a new constable starting work that day called Li-Neng and the police chief summoned him to his office.

'Li-Neng,' said the police chief, 'I have a very important job for you on your first day as a constable. Here is a warrant for the arrest of a dangerous criminal. Be off with you and do not return until you have captured him.'

When poor Li-Neng saw the tiger's name on the warrant, he shook with fright, but he was determined to make a good impression as a policeman and so he set off towards the mountains at once.

He had no idea how he was going to catch the tiger and he spent many days just wandering around without even seeing a trace of one. He began to feel very downhearted, but he was determined not to return empty-handed, so he pressed on. Further and further into the mountains he went until he came to a small lake into which a waterfall cascaded. It was such a pleasant spot that he decided to sit there for a while and rest. He lay back on the soft grass and listened to the sound of the rushing waterfall as it tumbled into the lake. It was so soothing that he soon fell into a deep sleep.

Suddenly, he was awakened by the feeling that he was being watched. He sat up and was so shocked by what he saw that he almost jumped out of his skin. Only a few feet away from him was a huge, fully grown tiger. He was just sitting there staring at him, blinking occasionally. Li-Neng

was terrified. He looked around for a means of escape, but all around were the steep walls of rock. So he decided to put a brave front and demanded, 'Are you the tiger who ate the young traveller who came this way last month?'

The tiger simply blinked and lay down. Li-Neng took this to mean yes, so he said, 'Then I arrest you in the name of the law. Will you come quietly?'

The tiger blinked again and rolled over on his back like a playful kitten, so Li-Neng plucked up all his courage, took a rope from his bag and tied it around the tiger's neck. 'Come along,' he said, 'Back to the town with you.'

The tiger did not resist his pull on the rope, but just walked alongside Li-Neng like an obedient dog. Li-Neng could hardly believe his luck and couldn't wait to see the look on the face of his chief when he arrived back with the tiger.

As he approached the town, everyone who saw him and the tiger ran away screaming with terror. The word spread rapidly ahead of him until it reached the ears of the police chief, who was in a meeting with the magistrate.

'What nonsense is this?' they both asked. In fact, they had both completely forgotten about the warrant for the tiger's arrest.

Suddenly, there was a commotion outside and they both went to see what it was all about. When they stepped on to the front porch of the police station, standing there before them was Li-Neng, with a huge tiger sitting next to him. All around the square the townsfolk were watching from upstairs windows or from the branches of trees where they had fled in terror when they saw Li-Neng coming into town with the tiger.

As soon as he saw the police chief, Li-Neng stood smartly to attention and saluted. 'I have arrested the tiger as you ordered, sir!' He held out the warrant, but the two men were transfixed with terror.

'W-well done, Li-Neng,' the police chief eventually stammered. 'How did you do it?'

Li-Neng was enjoying himself a great deal, but he tried to act as casually as possible. 'Oh, it wasn't very difficult,' he said nonchalantly. 'The tiger has confessed to the crime and has come quietly to face trial.'

'Trial!' blurted the magistrate, who had climbed on to the table by the doorway and was shaking like a leaf. 'Yes. . . . Yes, of course . . . bring the prisoner to the courthouse.'

A short while later the whole town watched as Li-Neng and the tiger sat in the dock and the magistrate, in his robes of office, said in a solemn voice, 'Tiger, you are charged with the murder of this woman's only son.' The magistrate pointed to the woman whose son had been killed. 'Do you confess to the crime?'

The tiger nodded his head slowly and blinked.

'Then I must sentence you,' said the magistrate. 'If you were a human, the sentence would almost certainly be death, but I must say that this case is most unusual. There is no record of a similar case in all my books of law. Therefore, I must think of a suitable punishment. As you are a tiger and obviously do not know much about the laws of man, and considering that you gave yourself up and came quietly, my sentence is as follows: you will go to the woman and try to make up to her for the loss of her son!'

At this, there was uproar in the courtroom. The woman was furious and demanded a retrial, but the magistrate said that his decision was final and that was the end of the matter.

Li-Neng took the tiger to the woman's house and untied the rope from around his neck. The tiger lay down in front of the house, and although the woman shouted abuse at him he just blinked at her, so eventually she gave up and went inside. That evening the tiger stood up and padded softly away into the darkness.

'Ah, I knew it!' said the woman. 'As if a tiger would do as the magistrate ordered! He has gone back to the mountains, no doubt to kill more innocent travellers.'

The next morning, however, when the woman opened her window and looked out, to her surprise there was the tiger. Lying in front of him was the body of a deer which he had obviously killed and carried there. The woman eyed the tiger and the deer suspiciously. 'Is that for me?' she asked. The tiger nodded and blinked.

Now, the woman had not eaten meat since the loss of her son as she could not afford to buy it, so she was soon tucking into a delicious venison stew which she shared with the tiger. Each day, from then on, the tiger returned with something to eat, sometimes it was a wild pig or a pheasant or another deer. He slept on the verandah outside the woman's door and kept her safe from thieves and robbers.

Soon the woman became fond of the great beast and he would place his head on her lap and purr loudly as she scratched his ears. He was like a son to her and, just as the magistrate had ordered he made up for the loss of her real son. Many years later the old woman died and the townsfolk gathered round her grave to pay their last respects. As they were doing so, the tiger appeared and the crowd parted as he trotted to the graveside. The tiger lifted his great head and roared once as if to say goodbye. Then he returned to the mountains and was never seen again.

Valiant Victor

Once upon a time, in India, there lived a weaver whose name was Victor. He was very small and skinny, and everyone laughed at him and teased him about his size. This upset poor Victor a great deal and he would get very angry. 'I may be small and skinny, but I have the courage of a tiger, and one day you will all see how brave and valiant I am,' he would say.

This just made everyone laugh at him even more and they started to call him Valiant Victor. But instead of being ashamed of his nickname, little Victor enjoyed it when people called out to him in the street, 'Hey, there goes Valiant Victor,' and soon he was known far and wide, although he had never done a brave act in his life.

One day Victor was sitting at his loom when a fly buzzed around his head. It was so annoying that Victor threw the shuttle he was using to weave the cloth at the irritating fly. To his surprise it hit the fly fair and square and killed it.

'There, you see,' cried Victor, 'that is how I handle creatures which annoy me, for I am the great Valiant Victor.'

The little man went all over the town telling everyone how he had killed the fly with a shuttle. Of course, everyone laughed at him, but he hardly noticed them, for he was far too busy boasting about his valiant deed. In fact, the more often he repeated the story the more he became convinced that he was the bravest man in the whole town, and finally he decided that it was high time he left and went to seek his fortune elsewhere. So the little weaver packed his bag and set off to find somewhere where his bravery would be appreciated.

Valiant Victor travelled for many days through many towns and villages until he came to a place where the local farmers were being plagued by a rogue elephant. The great beast was trampling their crops and terrifying their livestock. He had even attacked the farmers themselves when they tried to drive him off.

'Don't worry,' said Valiant Victor, 'I will sort out this elephant for you – I am the great Valiant Victor. Maybe you've heard of me?'

The farmers shook their heads; they hadn't heard of him and he didn't look as if he was capable of fighting a fully grown elephant, but they were willing to try anything to get rid of the beast. 'Hurrah for Valiant Victor,' they cheered, as the little man set off without even a weapon to fight with.

'That's the last we'll see of him,' they said, as he disappeared out of sight.

Soon Valiant Victor was alone in the part of the forest where the elephant had last been seen, and he began to stamp around loudly, shouting, 'Come on out, Elephant! Let me see you so that I can catch you.'

After a while there was a great noise of trees snapping and undergrowth being trampled, and at last the enormous elephant appeared. As soon as he saw the great beast, Valiant Victor stopped shouting. His courage deserted him and he turned and ran as fast as he could, with the angry elephant close behind. Suddenly the idea of being a great hero didn't seem so attractive to poor Victor as he looked over his shoulder at the charging elephant. The enraged beast was almost on top of him when Victor ran between two massive trees. The elephant followed at full speed, but then to Victor's relief he got jammed between the two tree trunks. Struggle as he might, the elephant was wedged tight and could not move.

After a while, the farmers cautiously ventured out to see if the little man had been trampled under foot, but to their amazement, there was Valiant Victor sitting a few feet away from the wedged elephant, who by now was so exhausted by his struggling that he was quite subdued. When the farmers asked Valiant Victor how he had managed to catch the elephant, he just shrugged. 'Oh, it was nothing,' he said casually.

It turned out that the elephant had had a nasty thorn embedded in his trunk and the pain had caused him to run amok. When the thorn was removed the elephant soon became his normal self and was released by the farmers to go back into the hills where the rest of the herd lived.

Well, the news spread about Valiant Victor and the elephant, and he was hailed as a hero by everyone. The people of the town asked him to stay and live with them, but Valiant Victor declined the kind invitation, saying that he was seeking fame and fortune and must carry on his journey.

So Valiant Victor left the town and continued to wander, not knowing where he was heading, until he came to a place that was being terrorized by a savage tiger. He would come in the night and make off with a calf or a goat, and the people were so afraid that they would lock themselves in their houses until daylight. When Valiant Victor heard this, he said, 'Have no fear, Valiant Victor is here, and I will catch the tiger!'

That night Valiant Victor waited in the darkness for the tiger to arrive and, sure enough, after a short wait he saw the great cat quietly padding towards him.

When the tiger saw Victor just standing there waiting,

he decided that he would make a fine meal. The tiger leapt into the air with a roar. It was then that Valiant Victor's courage deserted him and he turned and ran away as fast as he could. But the tiger simply took another great leap and almost grabbed the running Victor with his sharp claws. Unfortunately, the tiger didn't see the overhanging branch of a tree and he launched himself through the air with all his strength. He came to a sudden halt as his head smacked against the branch and he fell unconscious at Victor's feet. Victor could hardly believe his luck, for without a doubt the tiger would have killed him if it had not been for the branch.

Valiant Victor thought he had better do something before the tiger woke up, so he called out to the villagers who were hiding inside their houses: 'Come on out! I have knocked the tiger out with one blow; help me to tie it up!'

The people slowly opened their doors and came out one by one, and when they saw the tiger lying at Valiant Victor's feet they could hardly believe their eyes. They quickly brought a rope and tied the tiger's feet, and then took the animal to a cage ready to be taken to a zoo.

Of course, Victor was a hero and news of his daring deeds spread far and wide. As he continued on his way people would come out to see this great hero as he passed through their villages.

One day Valiant Victor came to the palace of a great rajah and he went up to the gates and said, 'Open the gates! Valiant Victor is here, and I wish to see the rajah!'

The gates were opened at once and the rajah came out to greet the famous Valiant Victor. 'Come in,' he said. 'I am honoured by your visit. Please stay here for as long as you wish.'

Valiant Victor liked the look of the palace so he decided

to rest there for a few weeks before going on with his travels. 'Thank you, Your Majesty,' he said, 'I don't mind if I do.'

He was made very comfortable in the palace and was waited on hand and foot by the rajah's servants, and as the days passed he became more and more settled. This is the life, he said to himself, I think I will settle down here and marry the rajah's pretty daughter.

The rajah was more than pleased to let Valiant Victor marry his daughter. After all, Victor was a great hero whose fame had spread across the land. So he was married to the beautiful princess and they lived in the palace in luxury for several months. Valiant Victor grew fat from all the lovely food he ate and became so lazy that he hardly ever left the palace. But one day the peace and quiet was broken by a messenger who rode into the palace courtyard with the news of an approaching army of brigands. The palace was in uproar as they had no means of defending themselves against such a threat.

The rajah sent for Victor and said, 'Thank goodness you are here, Valiant Victor. You will defend us, won't you?'

'Three cheers for Valiant Victor!' the people all cheered.

But Victor was not very happy about this; he had been lucky with the elephant and the tiger, but taking on a whole army of brigands was an entirely different matter. That night he decided it was time to leave the palace before the brigands surrounded it, so he went to his rooms and collected together all the valuable gold cups and plates he could find and put them into a sack. Then he crept quietly out of the gates and hurried away as fast as he could into the darkness.

What he didn't know was that the brigands were at that moment creeping quietly up the road towards the palace, hoping to take it by surprise. As Victor ran at full speed

round a bend in the road he went crashing headlong into the leading brigands. The gold plates and cups went clattering and crashing in every direction, making such a noise that the brigands thought they were under a full-scale attack from a terrible army. Victor screamed with terror but this only made the brigands think their leading group was being killed. There was so much confusion that the brigands set upon each other in the darkness and killed each other. The few who were left turned tail and ran away into the night.

When all the noise had died down, Victor crawled from under a bush where he had been hiding and looked around him. He bent down and picked up a sword that had been dropped by one of the brigands, and just then the rajah and his servants, who had come to see what all the noise was about, came round the corner. Well, you can imagine what they thought when they saw Victor standing there with a sword in his hand surrounded by the dead bodies of fifty or so brigands.

Victor was carried back to the palace shoulder high, and everyone came out to see the great hero who had fought an army of brigands single-handed. The rajah was so grateful that he gave Victor half of his wealth and made him heir to his throne.

So Valiant Victor, the luckiest hero in the world, lived happily ever after, and no one ever suspected that it was all because of luck that he was a hero at all.

The Metal Man

Once upon a time, in Africa, there lived a chief who was very powerful, but also very foolish. When he did foolish things, none of his advisers had the courage to tell him he was being foolish in case he had them thrown into prison.

One day the chief called all his advisers into his hut, where they all waited nervously for him to arrive. It wasn't long before the chief swept in and sat down on his chair.

'Last night', began the chief, 'I had a dream in which my enemies came and surrounded my kingdom. They came in such large numbers that our warriors were outnumbered by ten to one and it looked as if we would be defeated.' The chief paused for effect and the advisers shuffled about uncomfortably in the silence. Then he went on, 'Just as all seemed lost, a mighty warrior marched forth carrying my battle flag above his head, and the enemy turned and fled like cowards!'

At this, the advisers thought they had better do something, so they jumped up and down and cheered. This pleased the chief and he smiled cheerfully. Then one of the advisers stepped forward and cleared his throat before speaking: 'Ahem! Who was this mighty warrior, Sir?'

The chief was glad someone had asked that question for it was exactly what he had wanted. He rose to his feet. 'He was a METAL MAN!' he shouted triumphantly. 'The

spears and arrows of the enemy just bounced off him. He was invincible!'

The advisers clapped and cheered at this wonderful story, then they turned to each other, shook hands and slapped each other on the back. By the time the noise had eventually died down the chief was sitting on his chair again and when he had their full attention, he said, 'Go and fetch the blacksmith who made the fine jewellery for my wife. He must make me a metal man so that our kingdom will be safe from attack.'

Well, you could have heard a pin drop. The advisers just stood there with their mouths hanging open.

'Go on,' yelled the chief. 'Get on with it!'

At this, they all snapped out of their state of shock and ran in every direction, falling over each other in the process. 'Send for the blacksmith at once,' they all said, and a messenger was sent to the village where the man lived.

A short time later the blacksmith was escorted into the chief's hut. 'Good morning,' said the chief pleasantly. 'I have a very important task for you, blacksmith. I hope you will not let me down.'

Now the blacksmith thought the chief wanted him to make some more jewellery, so he replied, 'Have no fear, Sir, my work is of the highest standard. I will not let you down.'

'Good! Good!' said the chief. 'Here is what I want you to do. You must make me a man out of metal who can defend us against attack from our enemies, and you must do it quickly in case my dream was a warning that we are about to be attacked. Your reward will be a rich one, blacksmith, for this metal man will keep your countrymen safe for ever.'

Well, the poor blacksmith was so amazed that he didn't know what to say. He just nodded and left the hut as fast as he could. When he got outside he began to wonder just what he was going to do. It was impossible to do as the chief had asked, but if he admitted as much he would more than likely be thrown into prison.

All the way home the blacksmith tried to think of a way out of the terrible situation he was in, but to no avail. When he reached home he told his wife all about it.

'Why can't his advisers tell him what a foolish chief he is?' she cried. 'They should have the courage to stand up to him.'

The next morning the blacksmith went to his forge and sat down beside it feeling very lonely and miserable. Just then along came an old woman who had come to the village to sell herbs and potions to cure illnesses. 'What is wrong, blacksmith?' asked the woman. 'Perhaps I can help you.'

'I don't think so,' sighed the blacksmith, and he told her the whole sad story.

'Oh, I think I can help you there, you know,' chuckled the old woman. 'This is what you must do. You must go back to the chief and tell him that before you can make the metal man you will need some special ingredients that only he can supply. Ask him to order all his people to shave off all their hair and put it into baskets which are to be delivered to the village by noon tomorrow. Tell him that you need the hair to make a special fire to forge the metal for the metal man. Then tell him he must command all his people to cry into their buckets until they are full of tears and to bring those to the village by the following noon. Explain that you need the tears to quench the metal you are to use for the metal man.'

The blacksmith did as the old woman had said, although he could not see how it would help him. He went to the chief, who listened intently to what the blacksmith asked.

After a few moments the chief turned to the blacksmith

and said, 'I am sorry, but you cannot have the ingredients you ask for. I cannot order my subjects to shave all their hair off; and as for filling a bucket with tears, why, that is impossible! No, no, your request is foolish.'

'And so is yours, Sir,' said the blacksmith.

For a moment the chief looked as if he was going to explode with rage, but then a smile came over his face. 'You are right, blacksmith, I have been foolish. I asked for something impossible. It is quite clear that no one can make a living man from metal. You may go, and thank you for having the courage to tell me I was being foolish. As for my advisers, not one of them had the same courage and as a result they will all be dismissed immediately.'

The blacksmith went back to his village and thanked the old woman for helping him; he made her a special bracelet as a token of his gratitude.